Pete the Cat

Storybook Favorites

EASY STREET

Pete the Cat Storybook Favorites, originally published as *Pete the Cat Storybook Collection*
Copyright © 2016 by James Dean

Pete the Cat is a registered trademark of Pete the Cat, LLC © 2019 by James Dean

Pete the Cat: Pete's Big Lunch © 2013 by James Dean
Pete the Cat: Construction Destruction © 2015 by James Dean
Pete the Cat: Pete at the Beach © 2013 by James Dean
Pete the Cat: Cavecat Pete © 2015 by James Dean
Pete the Cat: Play Ball! © 2013 by James Dean
Pete the Cat: Robo-Pete © 2015 by James Dean
Pete the Cat: Too Cool for School © 2014 by James Dean

ISBN 978-0-06-289484-7

Typography by Jeff Shake
19 20 21 22 23 SCP 10 9 8 7 6 5 4 3 2 1

Pete the Cat
Storybook Favorites

by
James Dean

HARPER
An Imprint of HarperCollinsPublishers

Table of Contents

Pete the Cat
PETE'S BIG LUNCH

Here comes Pete!

It is lunchtime.

Pete is ready to eat.

What should Pete eat?

A sandwich would be nice.

Yes, Pete wants a sandwich.

Pete opens the fridge.

He takes out a loaf of bread.

He finds a yummy fish.

He adds tomato and mayo.

Pete looks at his sandwich.

It is too small.

Something is missing.

Pete knows what it needs.

His sandwich needs an apple.

Pete loves apples!

His sandwich needs crackers.

Crackers are crunchy.

Pete loves crunchy crackers!

Pete looks at his sandwich again.

It is still too small.

Pete is very hungry.

Pete adds a pickle.

Pete adds cheese.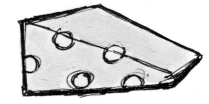

Pete adds an egg,

two hot dogs,

a banana,

and a can of beans.

Something is missing.

Pete adds ice cream!

He takes three huge scoops.

Pete's sandwich
is too big
for Pete to eat.

Pete wonders
what to do.
Pete thinks
and thinks.

"I've got it!" Pete says.

Pete calls all of his friends.

He asks them to come over.

Everyone goes to Pete's house.

They are all very hungry.

Pete shows them
his big lunch.

"Are you hungry?" asks Pete.
Pete's sandwich is big enough
for everyone.
"Dig in!" says Pete.

Pete's sandwich is good.

Pete's sandwich is VERY good.

Pete's sandwich is all gone.

Pete's friends are full.

They liked Pete's big lunch.

"Thanks for lunch,"
Pete's friends say.
"Thanks for sharing!"

"You're welcome," Pete says.
Sharing is cool.

Pete the Cat

Construction Destruction

"Recess!" Pete shouts as the bell rings. But when Pete gets outside to play—oh no. The playground is a disaster. The swings are broken, the slide is rusty, and the sandbox is full of weeds.

Pete makes plans for a new playground.

"Wow!" says Principal Nancy. "Can you really build that?"

"Not by myself," says Pete. "I'm going to need some help."

"Whatever you need, Pete, it's yours."

The next day, Pete arrives at the playground before school. The construction crew is already there. He gives them the go-ahead to tear down the old playground.

Creak! Crash!

Down goes the slide.

Clink! Clank!

Down go the swings.

Bang! Boom! Down goes the tower.

Honk! Honk! A truck arrives to recycle the metal.

44

The new playground equipment has arrived. It's time to get to work. The cement mixer will pour concrete. The dump truck will bring sand and dirt. The backhoe will dig. The whole team will get the job done.

46

Building a playground is hard work.

The new playground is cool, but it's not cool enough.
"What do you think?" Pete asks, holding up his latest plans.
"It will be too hard to build," says one of the workers.
"And everything is almost finished," says another.

"But it will make this the best playground ever," Pete says.
"Then let's do it," the workers say.

50

Screwdrivers twist in screws. Wrenches tighten the nuts. The workers try to make everything perfect.

Hooray!

The new playground is ready.

52

"Oh no!" says Principal Nancy as the new playground crashes to the ground. "The pieces are all mixed up."

Everyone is disappointed—except for Pete.

"It's not how we planned it!" Pete shouts.
"It's even better!"

56

This playground is filled with surprises and places to explore. The school playground is the most amazing playground ever.

Sometimes you've got to dare to dream big.

Pete the Cat

Pete at the Beach

It is a hot day!

Pete the Cat goes to the beach
with his mom and his brother, Bob.

"Let's go in the water,"
Bob says.

"Maybe later," says Pete.

Bob likes to surf.

He rides the big waves.

It looks like fun.

"I'm hot," says Pete.

"Go in the water," says Mom.

"Maybe later," says Pete.

Pete makes a sand castle.

His mom helps him dig.

Here comes a big wave.

And there goes Pete.

Oh, no!

Where did his sand castle go?

Bob rides a big wave.

"Wow!" says Pete.

"That looks like fun."

Pete and his mom take a walk.

They find seashells.

They see a crab.

Pete's feet get wet.

His feet feel cool.

The rest of him is hot.

It is time for lunch.

Pete eats a sandwich.

He drinks lemonade.

The sun is very hot.

And Pete is very, very hot.

Bob is wet and cool.

"Let's play ball," says Pete.

"No, thanks," says Bob.

"I want to surf."

Pete throws the ball.

His mom catches it.

"Let's get our feet wet,"
says Mom.
"Well, okay," says Pete.

The water is cool.

It feels good.

Pete goes in deeper.

Bob waves to Pete.
"I want to show you
how to surf!" he yells.

Pete does not say

"Maybe later."

He says, "Let's do it!"

"Lie on the board," says Bob.
Pete lies on the board.

"Paddle," says Bob.

Pete paddles out.

He waits for a big wave.

A big wave is coming!

"Stand up!" says Bob.

Pete stands up.

Then Pete falls down.
It was scary,
but it did not hurt.

"Try again later," says Bob.

Pete wants to try again now.

Pete lies down again.

He paddles out and waits.

Here comes a wave!

Pete stands up.

This time he rides the wave!

"Good job," says Bob.

Pete wants to surf all day.

Bob does, too.

So they take turns.

Pete and Bob rock and roll
with the waves.
What a great day!

It is okay to be afraid.

But it is more fun to surf!

Pete the Cat

Cavecat Pete

90

Cavecat Pete wakes up early. The sun is shining. The birds are singing.

Today is going to be a great day, Pete thinks. But then Pete's bed starts to shake. His friend Vinny the Velociraptor is coming to visit.

"It's a perfect day for a picnic!" says Vinny.

"What a great idea," says Pete. "Who should we invite?"

"Everyone!" Vinny yells.

"Right on!" says Pete.

Pete loves picnics! He heads out to invite
all his friends.

First Pete finds his good friend Ethel the Apatosaurus!

To get her attention, Pete climbs all the way up to the top of the tallest tree.

94

"Would you like to come to a picnic?" Pete asks.
"I'd love to," says Ethel. "What can I bring?"
"How about a really big salad?" Pete suggests.
"What a great idea," says Ethel. "I'm on it!"

95

Pete wanders along the river. He sees T. rex!
T. rex plays guitar. T. rex is awesome!

"Hey, T. rex," Pete yells, "want to come to a
picnic?"

"Sweet," says T. rex. "Can I bring my guitar?"

"Definitely," says Pete. "We can jam!"

"Count me in," says T. rex. "Okay if I bring
Al the Allosaurus? He's a whiz on the drums."

"The more the merrier," says Pete.

Pete sees his friend Terri the Pterosaur in the sky.
"Hi, Pete!" she calls.

Pete invites Terri to the picnic, too. "Would you mind giving me a lift?" Pete asks.
"Sure," says Terri. "Climb aboard."

Pete sees the spiked tail of his main man Skip the Stegosaurus.

"How are you feeling today, Skip?" Pete asks. Skip has been sick with the sniffles.

"Better," says Skip. "Thanks for asking."

"You up for a picnic?"

"I think so," says Skip. "I'd hate to miss the fun."

It's almost time for the picnic! Cavecat Pete rushes through the forest. He doesn't want to be late. Whoops! Pete trips over Trini the Triceratops.

"We're playing hide-and-seek," she says before Pete can ask what she was doing. "I think I hid a little too well."

"How long have you been there?" asks Pete.

"What's today?" asks Trini.

"Well, all the dinosaurs are going to be at the picnic grounds. Want to come?" Pete asks.

"What a great idea! Maybe somebody there will play hide-and-seek with me!"

It's time for the picnic. Vinny and Ethel are setting up the picnic tables. T. rex and Al are warming up to play some tunes. Terri and Trini are playing hide-and-seek. Even Skip seems to be enjoying himself!

"It doesn't get any better than this," Pete says.

T. rex comes over then. "Hey, Pete," he asks, "is there anything else to eat? I'm a carnivore. I don't eat salad."

Trini comes over. "Terri is cheating at hide-and-seek. She's flying around and peeking."

Skip comes over. "I don't feel so good," he says, and he sneezes.

104

The dinosaurs all start to argue. The picnic will be ruined if Pete doesn't do something. He leans over to Al and says, "Can you give me a beat?" Pete takes out his guitar, and he starts to sing.

Before long, everyone is having a great time.
"You know," T. rex tells Ethel, "I've never
actually tried salad before."
"Try it," says Pete. "I bet you'll like it."

T. rex tastes the salad. Crunch, crunch, crunch.
"Yum!" says T. rex. "This salad is delicious!"
Everyone grabs a plate and digs in.

Everyone decides to play hide-and-seek.
Pete is happy that everyone is getting along.
He feels lucky to have such great friends.

109

"This was the best picnic ever," everyone agrees.
"It was the best picnic because you guys are the best friends ever," Pete says.
And no one can argue with that.

Pete the Cat

PLAY BALL!

Here comes Pete the Cat.

Pete has a mitt.

He has a bat and a ball.

What will Pete do today?

Pete will play baseball!

Today is the big game.

The Rocks are playing the Rolls.

Pete and his team get set.

They play catch.

They take turns hitting.

It is time to play ball!

The Rocks bat first.

Pete waits for his turn.

Crack! The batter hits the ball.

He runs to first base.

"Way to go!" Pete cheers.

"Batter up!" says the umpire.
Pete goes up to bat.

The pitcher throws the ball.
Pete swings the bat.

He misses the ball.
Strike one!

The pitcher pitches again.

Pete swings too high.

Strike two!

The pitcher winds up.

He throws.

Pete strikes out.

But Pete is not sad.

He did his best.

Pete's friend Ben is up.

Ben hits a home run!

"Way to go!" cheers Pete.

The Rolls
go up to bat.
The Rocks go to the field.

Crack! Here comes a fly ball!

"I've got it!" calls Pete.

The ball hits his mitt.

But Pete drops it.

He is not sad.

He did his best.

Another hit!
This time Pete catches it,
but he throws it too far.

Pete is up at bat again.

He wants to hit the ball.

The first pitch is too low.

Pete does not swing.

Ball one!

The next pitch is too high.

Pete does not swing.

Ball two!

The third pitch is inside.

The fourth pitch is outside.

Pete gets four balls.

Pete wanted to get a hit.

But a walk is cool, too.

The next batter gets a hit.

Pete runs as fast as he can.

Pete wants to score,

but he is out at home plate.

Pete is not sad.

He did his best.

The game is over.

The Rocks win six to three!

"Way to go!" calls Pete.

"Good game," the Rocks say.

"Good game," the Rolls say.

Pete did his best.

He had fun.

What a great game!

Pete the Cat

Robo-Pete

What a great, sunny morning! Pete can't wait to play baseball with his friends.

"Do you want to play catch?"
Pete asks Larry.
  "I can't," says Larry.
"I'm going to the library."

"Do you want to play catch?"
Pete asks Callie.
  "I was about to go for a
bike ride," says Callie.

"Do you want to play catch?" Pete asks John.
"I can't right now," says John. "I have to paint the fence."

Pete wishes his friends would do what he wants to do. It's no fun playing catch all by himself.
If only I knew another me . . . , Pete thinks. And like that, Pete has a great idea!

Pete builds a robot! He programs it to be just like him.

"Welcome to the world, Robo-Pete!" Pete says to the robot. "You're my new best friend. We'll do everything together."

"And I want to play catch," says Pete.
"Great idea!" says Robo-Pete.

Pete and Robo-Pete play catch.

"Wow!" says Pete, running after the ball. "You sure can throw far!"

Robo-Pete throws farther and farther until . . .

"Time out!" says Pete as he tries to catch his breath.
"Let's play something else."
"I want to play whatever you want to play,"
Robo-Pete says proudly.

"How about we play hide-and-seek?" says Pete.
"That will be fun," says Robo-Pete.

Pete finds the best hiding place ever! He's sure Robo-Pete will never find him.

"Ten, nine, eight, seven, six, five, four, three, two, one!" shouts Robo-Pete. "Ready or not, here I come!"

"Gotcha!" shouts Robo-Pete, tagging Pete.
"Hey, how did you find me?" says Pete.
"With my homing device," says Robo-Pete.
"I can find anyone, anywhere."

"Okay, enough hide-and-seek," says Pete. "Let's play some guitar."

Pete teaches Robo-Pete how to play a song he made up.

"You have to feel the music,"
Pete explains.
"Okay," says Robo-Pete.

"To feel it, I need to play loud," explains Robo-Pete.

Pete tries to stop Robo-Pete, but Robo-Pete can't hear him over the noise. . . .

"This is fun," says Robo-Pete.

"This is awful!" says Pete the Cat.

"Okay," says Robo-Pete. "Let's ride our skateboards instead."

Before Pete can answer, Robo-Pete's feet transform into a motorized skateboard with super speedy wheels.

"Let's go!"
Robo-Pete shouts.

"Wait!" calls Pete.

Pete chases after Robo-Pete. He has no idea where Robo-Pete is going.

156

Robo-Pete crashes into the sandbox at the playground.
"Are you okay?" Pete asks his robot.

"I am a robot. I am indestructible!" says Robo-Pete.
"What is this strange place?"
"It's a playground," says Pete. He waves to his friends.

"This is Robo-Pete," Pete says to Callie, Larry, and John.
"I made him myself."
"Cool," says Larry.

"We are going to help John finish painting," says Callie.
"And then we are going bike riding."
"I want to go on the slide!" interrupts Robo-Pete.

"Robo-Pete, I want to help my friends paint the fence!"
Pete tells his robot.

"Paint the fence—that would be great," Robo-Pete says.
"I am programmed to paint faster than anyone."

Pete and his friends try to help, but Robo-Pete paints too fast.

So instead they ride bikes,

and they read books . . .

and after Robo-Pete is done painting,
they help him clean the brushes.

Pete realizes that it doesn't matter what they do.
Just being with his friends is what makes it fun!

Pete wants to look cool.

He asks everyone,

"What should I wear?"

"Wear your yellow shirt,"
his mom says.
"It is my favorite."

So Pete does.

"Wear your red shirt,"
Pete's friend Marty says.
"It is my favorite."

So Pete does.

"Wear your blue shirt,"
Pete's brother Bob says.
"It is my favorite."

So Pete does.

"Wear your long pants,"
Pete's teacher says.
"They are my favorite."

2+2=4

So Pete does.

"Wear the shorts with the fish,"
Pete's friend Callie says.
"They are my favorite."

So Pete does.

"Wear the polka-dot socks,"
the bus driver says.
"They are my favorite."

So Pete does.

"Wear the cowboy boots," Grumpy Toad says.

"They are my favorite."

So Pete does.

"Wear the tie with the stripes," Emma says.

"It is my favorite."

So Pete does.

"Wear your baseball hat,"
his coach says.
"It is my favorite."

So Pete does.

Pete puts on all the clothes.

Does he look cool?

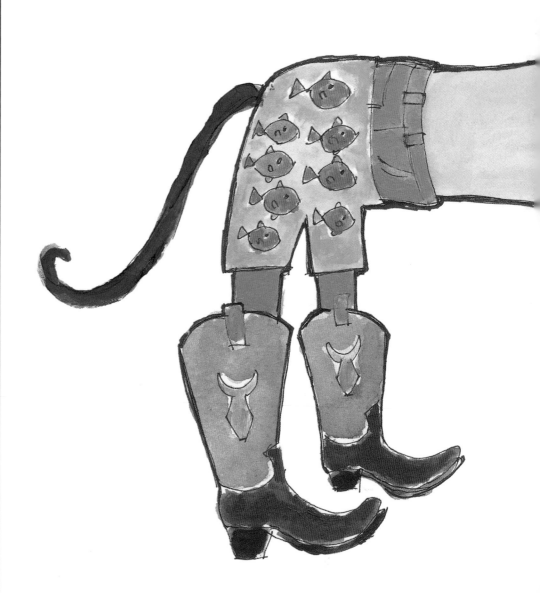

No.

Pete looks silly.

He also feels very hot!

Pete goes home.

He changes his clothes.

Pete puts on HIS favorite shirt.

Pete puts on HIS favorite pants.

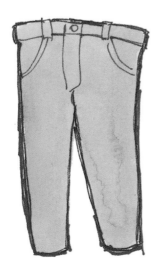

Pete puts on HIS favorite socks.

Pete puts on HIS favorite shoes.

Pete puts on his sunglasses.

Pete says, "Now I am COOL."